To Chase Christmas '03

Love,

Dianna & Daddad

THE NUTCRACKER

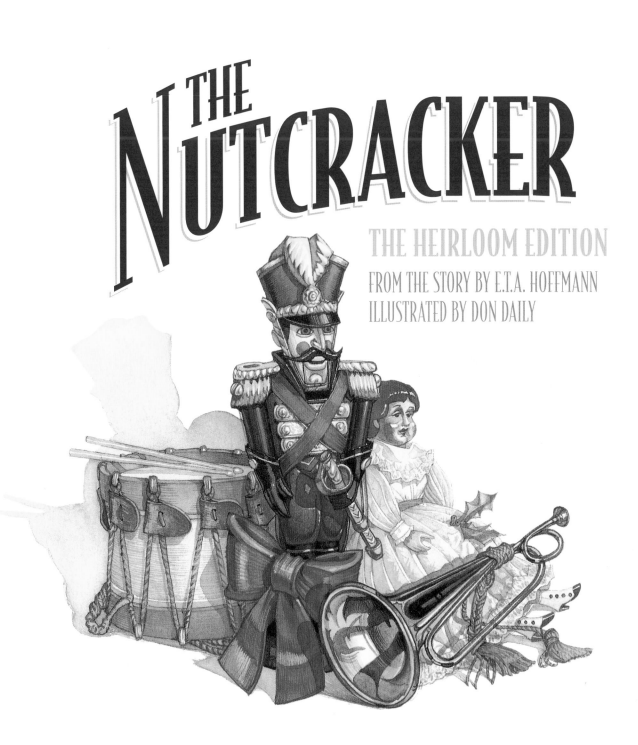

THE HEIRLOOM EDITION

FROM THE STORY BY E.T.A. HOFFMANN

ILLUSTRATED BY DON DAILY

RUNNING PRESS

PHILADELPHIA · LONDON

I would like to thank:

My daughter, Susie, for her lively portrayal of Maria, and her princely

brother, Joe; my wife, Renee, who made the costumes used in this story, and whose insight

and encouragement made these pictures possible; my friends and models—

Donna, Mark, Jim, Randee, and Matthew.

—DON DAILY

Printed in China

9   8   7   6   5   4   3   2   1
Digit on the right indicates the number of this printing

Library of Congress Control Number: 2003090669
ISBN 0-7624-1668-8

Cover design by Bill Jones
Interior design by Rosemary Tottoroto
Adapted by Daniel Walden
Edited by Joelle Herr
Typography: Bodega Serif and Garamond

This book may be ordered by mail from the publisher.
Please include $2.50 for postage and handling.
But try your bookstore first!

Published by Running Press Book Publishers
125 South Twenty-second Street
Philadelphia, Pennsylvania 19103-4399

Visit us on the web!
www.runningpress.com

CONTENTS

INTRODUCTION

Have you ever loved a toy so much you wished it came to life? Did you dream of the exciting adventures you would have with your special friend? If so, you are not the only one. Nearly two hundred years ago, in 1815, the German writer E. T. A. Hoffmann wrote a story called *The Nutcracker and the Mouse King*, telling how a little girl's love brought to life her cherished Nutcracker, an enchanted Christmas gift from her mysterious godfather.

The tale charmed readers of all ages, including the French writer Alexandre Dumas, who published a retelling of the story in 1847. From that adaptation, the Russian composer Peter Ilich Tchaikovsky and the choreographer Lev Ivanov created their ballet, *The Nutcracker.* First performed in St. Petersburg in 1892, it is now a classic performed throughout the world every holiday season.

Why has *The Nutcracker* remained so popular? As the story itself explains, "If you love something very much, it is always alive." Pure love of this extraordinary story has kept the words alive for nearly two hundred years, so they can dance for you across these colorful pages.

CHAPTER ONE

It had been snowing all day, and the gray city of Frankfurt was transformed. From her bedroom window Maria Stahlbaum watched the white flakes falling across the chimneys and tiled roofs, whirling against dark windows, and laying a thick carpet down every street and alley. The wind was rising, frequently blowing the snow in layers so dense as to hide the houses opposite. Then the layers would open and you could see every lintel and cornice growing bigger with the snow.

Presently lamps were lighted in the windows next door, and in the bright beams the driven snowflakes surged up like a crowd of elfin dancers in ballet dress. Waltzing and following fast behind each other, they moved on in a mighty leap straight across the space toward Maria's window. She heard the tinkle of tiny diamonds upon the panes. She saw the fairylike figures, just for a moment, before a great blast of wind shook the old house and threw a blanket of snow against the glass.

Luckily, Maria thought, the fir tree had been brought to the door that morning—for it was Christmas Eve—the party gifts had all been wrapped and the good things to eat prepared or delivered. But how would the guests ever get here

through such a storm? There was to be a dance in the big room at the back of the house, and Maria could not bear to miss any of the ladies in their evening dresses.

And what of old Papa Drosselmeyer? He was godfather to both Maria and her brother Fritz. Christmas would not be Christmas without Godfather Drosselmeyer! Such a strange old man, so wise and so clever. So severe at times, in his black formal clothes, his old-fashioned manners, and grave voice. For years he had worn a dark patch over one eye— but the other eye was as staring and sharp as an owl's. And yet Maria and Fritz loved him completely. No one else could tell such exciting stories, or bring such a feeling of wonder to every part of the festivities. And his presents were fantastic beyond belief—and each one made by himself. It was almost as if he were a magician!

Last year he had brought them a toy castle on a hill above a moat, and when you turned a crank a troop of knights rode up to the gate.

Then the drawbridge was lowered, the great door opened, and out came a princess to receive her guests. Before that, one year, there had been a magic theater with two scenes from Sleeping Beauty acted out by tiny figures. And other inventions so precious that Father had a special cupboard built to keep them safe behind glass doors. That cupboard, too, stood in the big room downstairs where the Christmas party always took place.

Maria unlatched the window and pushed it open against the snow piled on the sill. The icy, white powder rushed up into her face, but as she leaned out a little she could see people with lanterns coming down the street. There were four grown-ups and several children. All of them were bundled tight in heavy coats. They looked funny because their feet were almost buried in the soft snow. Beyond them was another group of people. Surely that was her Aunt Lisa in the scarlet greatcoat! All of them were coming toward Maria's house. Soon she and Fritz would be summoned to the big room, and the wonderful Christmas party would begin.

Suddenly Maria felt herself lifted from behind by two strong arms. She struggled and kicked backward and came down in the room with a thud. She had scooped up a fistful of snow and now she held it menacingly toward her brother Fritz. He was always playing tricks like that. But he let her go, to dodge the snowball, which broke on the carpet behind him.

"Ria," he said, "Mr. and Mrs. Kretchmas have come, and Mr. and Mrs. Krone, with all their children, and the whole Zimmerman family. Come down the back stairs! You can see the grown-ups trimming the tree through the keyhole of the side door. The tree is the best we've ever had . . . and I think I have a real cannon . . . and you have a doll with a big moustache!"

"You're making it up! No doll has a moustache."

"This one does, and a blue hat with a plume. It's a man doll, I guess, and I think he has a long sword . . . he must be a general."

"You're crazy! Who ever heard of a general doll?"

"I saw it," Fritz said. "And at any rate there is a table loaded with food—chocolate cake, ginger cookies, and heaps of peppermint stripes and all-colored bon-bons. Come on!"

"Has Godfather come?"

"Godfather never comes at the beginning. Don't you remember?"

"But will he come through this storm? He's so old and wrinkled . . . and then he has only one good eye."

"He'll come all right . . . with some mad present that has to be kept locked up. The snow won't keep him away. You know, I think he can fly like an owl and see in the dark. How he scares me sometimes! I'll bet he could fly right through that window. . . . Look out, here he comes!"

"Whoo—whoo," the blizzard shrieked against the windowpane. A chunk of solid snow dropped unexpectedly from the roof like a white owl upon the ledge outside. Fritz ran

and locked the window tight, then grabbed his sister's hand, and the children rushed laughing out of the room.

A mouse scurried out of sight as Maria and Fritz hurried down the hall. Dr. Stahlbaum's house was old and huge and there were a number of mice in the walls, but he was too kind-hearted to trap them. Fritz did not mind them at all. But ever since Maria had seen one running off with a little rug from her doll house she did not like them. They were big, blackish mice, too, and having such kind-hearted people to live with had made them very bold. Sometimes at night, most often when the moon was shining, Maria would be wakened by the faint but persistent *cranch, cranch* of a mouse gnawing a hole in the wall behind her bureau.

There was a broad, steep stairway going down to the family rooms on the floors below. On the ground floor, running out like a wing into the garden, was the largest room in the house. It was a kind of drawing-room and play-room combined. You could reach it

through the main hall and you could also reach it by way of the back stairs, which was the way Fritz and Maria now took.

When this house was built, long ago, doors often had keyholes as big as your middle finger, and since this door was a double one, the keyhole was extra large. At first, as Maria looked, everything was blurred by people moving back and forth as busy as squirrels, each one adding some bit to the preparations. The carpet had been rolled back for dancing. Along the right side was a long table spread with platters and raised dishes of all kinds of food.

Behind and above the people, in front of one window and nearly as tall, rose the Christmas tree. Its dark and beautiful branches curved out into the room, layer above layer, adorned with marvelous little toys, with fairy-tale angels and birds, with flowers of spun glass, and with amusing cotton kittens and gnomes and animals of all kinds—so many that you could not possibly count them. And, in much the way that snow might lie on a fir tree in the forest, a frosting of silver tinsel dripped from bough to bough in even curves, growing smaller as the tree narrowed upward. Near the top was a figure of Father Christmas, and at the very top a star.

"Isn't the tree wonderful!" Maria exclaimed.

Clara and Karl were only two of several cousins who had come to the Christmas Eve party here. But they also knew about the side door to the great room and now came running in upon Fritz and Maria.

"Merry Christmas!" they called. "Oh, you're peeking! Let me look. Let me look."

And, pushing and shoving, as overhasty people do, they all tried to look through the keyhole, no one having time enough to catch more than a blurred image before another child was close upon him trying to see, and finally all of them falling on

top of one another in a mad scramble of giggles and acrobatics. They would have rolled in a heap, right into the room, had the door been suddenly opened.

Just then the clock struck seven and the children heard Mrs. Stahlbaum calling: "Children, Father Christmas has come!"

They had just managed to disentangle themselves, to stand up and smooth out their party clothes when the doors were thrown open wide. Maria's mother stood inside with her arms extended. "Merry Christmas, my darlings," she said.

The tree had been lighted. Its glow and its fragrance filled the room. At the top of the tree the star shone; every ornament twinkled.

"Merry Christmas," the children said softly.

CHAPTER TWO

I t was the custom for the children to have a little dance first, and then for the grown-ups to have a waltz, and then for young and old to dance together. Between dances they had glasses of punch, and Maria helped her mother pass the little cups around.

She did not see Godfather Drosselmeyer. She kept looking, too, for the strange man doll that Fritz had described—but there was nothing like that among her many presents. And now she was far too busy passing the cold meat and sandwiches and little cakes to think about her gift. But quite suddenly, as she offered a slice of cake to old Mrs. Gumpel, who was sitting close to the tree, Maria saw the most remarkable thing.

Fritz had been telling the truth. Standing stiffly on a little table, as if at attention, was a little soldier. He wore highly polished boots, red trousers with a blue stripe, a white vest crossed by two bands of crimson, a deep blue general's coat, and an impressive hat with a plume. He must be made out of some kind of metal, Maria thought, for he looked so sturdy and strong. He had a high-arched nose, a

jutting chin, and round and brave-looking eyes. A rather extra-large moustache grew from his upper lip. He held a long sword at his left side, and his eyes had such a trusting and noble expression—brave and gentle at the same time—that Maria lost her heart to him at once.

Why, he is like a little prince! she thought. The soldier looked up at her steadily. His painted eyelashes gave him a very alert and appealing expression, like a big dog begging for a piece of your cake. How could anyone resist him? He made you feel protective and brave yourself.

". . . Thank you, child," she heard Mrs. Gumpel saying. "The almond torte is delicious. . . ."

The clock struck again, and as it did so the door to the big hall opened slowly, and there stood Godfather Drosselmeyer. He was dressed all in black, with a gold chain around his neck. His white cravat and his hair like spun silver made the black suit look very somber. He always wore a black patch over his left eye, but his other eye was so bright and piercing that it well served him for two. His usually white face was flushed with a rosy glow from the snowy night. When he came forward, he was followed by two tiny, little menservants, each carrying a Christmas package nearly as big as a big boy. No one had seen such large packages before. When the greetings were over, the two servants untied and opened the packages. Out of one box they took a huge cabbage, out of the other a very pink cake. Everyone crowded around in astonishment and curiosity.

The servants then lifted the cabbage and the cake, and underneath each was a doll nearly three feet tall, and almost real-looking. They were dressed as a shepherd and shepherdess. Then they seemed to come alive! The dolls rose and bowed to the audience and then to each other, and executed a most graceful and charming dance. They ended by bowing low and sitting again in position ready for the green cabbage and pink cake to cover them.

Everyone was delighted and charmed by the performance.

When they had vanished under their covers, Godfather Drosselmeyer came over to Maria and Fritz. He kissed each of them and said:

"My dear godchildren, these creations were made for you. They come to wish you a Happy Christmas, to give you old Drosselmeyer's love."

"Thank you, Godfather," they said together, "and Merry Christmas to you."

Drosselmeyer took Maria's hand affectionately. "I sent you and Fritz another little gift," he said. "Have you seen it? No? Well, look here!"

He went across toward the tree, past old Mrs. Gumpel, who was still munching sweet cakes, and picked up the brave, iron soldier.

"Oh, I love him, Godfather!" Maria cried.

"He is a nutcracker," said Papa Drosselmeyer. "Look! His jaws are so strong that he can crack the hardest nut without hurting his teeth at all."

Papa Drosselmeyer held the soldier with one hand and with his other raised the sol-dier's long sword backward. As he did so the mouth opened wide, revealing two rows of very white teeth. Then Drosselmeyer placed a walnut in the nutcracker's mouth, pressed down the sword, and the jaw closed, cracking the shell into four even pieces. He handed the cracked nut to Maria. Then he tried a hazel-nut, an almond, and a Brazil nut, each time giving the opened nut to one little girl or another. The boys, too, had crowded around to see this curious fellow. But Fritz was not much impressed.

"Didn't I tell you, Maria?" he said. "Now you have a doll with a big, black moustache!"

"He's not a doll. He's a magic nutcracker."

"What's so magic about him?" Fritz asked. He had never seen a nutcracker shaped like a soldier, but he had seen silver ones and wooden ones with springs.

"Let me have him," he demanded. "I'll bet he can't crack every nut."

"No, you'll hurt him. Godfather, please don't give Nutcracker to Fritz."

"But I brought him for both of you my dear. There Fritz . . . and be careful. He'll crack your nuts for years, but you must not abuse him."

Thereupon Godfather Drosselmeyer turned away to speak with some older friends. Fritz held the little soldier high in the air and started putting nuts in his mouth and crushing them, one right after another. *Crack, crack, crack, crack* went the little jaws, and nut after nut fell out perfectly bitten into four pieces. Then Fritz became annoyed and took an exceptionally large and heavy hickory nut, the toughest he could find, and pushed it far back into the soldier's mouth. *Crack, crack, crack,* . . . Fritz banged the sword up and down. The nut fell out, its shell broken in four even pieces, but there was a loose, clanking sound. The little mouth fell open again, though no one had lifted the sword. Nutcracker was badly hurt.

"Fritz, you did it on purpose! You hurt him on purpose! How unhappy he looks now!"

Maria was dreadfully upset. Fritz laughed,

to cover his shame, and turned away. But Maria took Nutcracker up in her arms and tried again and again to get his lower jaw into position. For Nutcracker seemed more real to her than did any of her dolls, and she felt certain he was in pain. What would she do now?

Papa Drosselmeyer had been watching her from across the room. He came over and shook his head. Gently he took up Nutcracker and tried to set the broken jaw, but it was no use.

"He is badly hurt, Maria," he said. "But perhaps we can heal the wound in time. Let us bandage it well and give him some rest."

Taking a large linen handkerchief from his coat pocket, Drosselmeyer bound it firmly around the jaw, holding it in position as he did so.

"With love and good care he should recover. Now put him down and enjoy the rest of the party."

Maria went to the toy cupboard, where one of her doll's beds stood on the lowest shelf. It was just the right size for Nutcracker. Gently, she made him comfortable in the bed, and she was not at all surprised when his eyes closed as she laid him down. He had no fever, she could tell. He could sleep now. In the morning she would come to look after him and bring him some nourishment.

Meanwhile the party had become very merry. People were laughing and talking gaily. Coming back from the cupboard, Maria saw that the presents had just been given. For each girl a handsomely dressed doll, with a doll's blanket and pillow. For each boy a little rifle, and either a drum or a fife. Soon the girls were rocking their new babies in their arms, and the boys, led by Fritz, formed into a platoon of well-drilled troops and went parading back and forth across the room. Shrill fifes pierced the air and drum rolls thundered out over all conversation. On they came, in full battle array, and suddenly making a left-march, they plunged head-on into the group of girls with their dolls. Maria started scolding Fritz, and in two minutes there was more noise in the room

than in the wild storm outside.

At length Fritz's father could tolerate it no longer. "Stop it, stop it!" he cried. "This is a party for everyone, not just for boys and girls. Come all of you and take partners. We need another dance."

Aunt Lisa sat at the square piano, and soon they were all off in a lively polka. It was great fun, and had to be followed by an easier waltz. Then the ices and rich mocha cake were served, with hot chocolate for the children. Some of the grown-ups had wine, and they offered toasts to each other and to Christmas itself. They stood in front of the tree and sang the carol of Christmas Night.

And then it was time to be going. Old Mrs. Gumpel was already nodding, and several boys were struggling to keep from yawning. The warm room, the rich food, and the dancing had made everyone tired. So into their winter wraps and out into the snowy night they went, with such fond farewells that you would have thought there is no time so wonderful as

Christmas—and you would have been right.

The last to come was the last to leave. Long after the children were in their beds, Mother and Father stood in the front hall saying good-night to the lingering guests. It was getting chilly from the constant opening of the outer door. Only when everyone else had gone did Godfather Drosselmeyer appear—at the far end of the hall, not from the cloak room, although he was covered from shoulders to shoes in an immense gray fur coat. There was a crafty glint in his eye and a smile on his face.

"Well, you have made an old man feel young again," Papa Drosselmeyer said to his hosts. "What a splendid and joyous party! I have not spent a more enjoyable evening in many a year. Truly, a spell was put upon this house tonight."

He shook hands with Dr. Stahlbaum, put on his tall fur hat, and stood on the top step. The snowstorm swirled down around him and he seemed to vanish in it like a wizard.

Days later a maid, who had come back into the empty party room that night to tidy up a bit after all the guests had gone, said she had been badly frightened by finding an old man there in the corner, bending over a doll's bed. He had a slender shining object in one hand, like a medicine dropper or a small screw-driver. When she called out to him he just raised one finger to his lips and made the sign of silence. In the dim room the maid was too startled to know if it was one of the guests—she thought it could not possibly be.

CHAPTER THREE

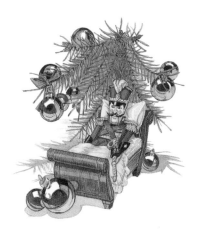

Cranch, cranch . . . cranch . . . there was that sound in the walls again. Maria sat up in bed, holding the quilt around her. How cold it was. She leaned from her bed to look at the sky. The snow had stopped falling and the moon had come out. She could see it glinting on the tiny, tinsel wrapper of a candy on her bed table. She had brought it up for a goodnight snack and had been too sleepy to eat it. She felt wide awake now, though she could not have slept very long, for it was deep night.

Cranch, cranch—they were louder than ever. Were they bigger mice? Or were there more of them?

She thought of the Christmas tree and of Nutcracker lying in his little bed with its thin cover. She wished she had brought him up here. Surely she should have given him more covers, for the party room would be bitterly cold by now.

Maria slid out of bed, and into her slippers and wrapper. When she lighted her bedside candle-lamp, the sound in the walls stopped abruptly. She opened the door quietly and went down the long, dark hall toward the stairs. Maria's velvet

slippers muffled her steps. The stairs were carpeted and firm and she went down them in complete silence.

Even going into the big room made no sound, for the door was ajar and she could pass through. Most of the room lay in shadow; her candle beam lighted only a narrow strip of the floor. As she came in it followed across the wall, up the tall owl-clock. It picked out the dial and then both golden hands pointing together to the owl's head on top.

The owl stirred and opened its eyes, and at that very instant, the clock spoke—a loud, deep, and hollow *O-o-o-o* that echoed from wall to wall. The owl raised itself up and began beating its wings. The clock struck again, and again, as Maria went on to the toy cupboard. In front of it was the doll's bed. And there was Nutcracker sound asleep. To her great joy, his mouth was peacefully closed and the bandage had slipped off. He would get well!

She started to take him up in her arms . . . and there came that sound, faintly, *cranch,*

cranch, cranchety-cranch.

The sound came again, closer and louder: *cranch, cranch!* It was followed by the rattle of tiny running feet.

A mouse's face appeared under the Christmas tree, and vanished. Then another one, much nearer. Oh what a big and ugly mouse! He seemed to be getting larger and coming straight for Maria.

At this moment her candle went out. A score of wicked little mouse eyes danced around the room. Terrified, Maria threw herself on the sofa and buried her face in the pillows.

When she looked out again there was a strange dim light all over the room. She could not tell where it came from. Mice—large, fat, and nearly black mice, with long and stringy tails—were moving back and forth in a kind of planned activity, as if following orders. They had sharp, little knives like swords, and they were assembling on the side of the room opposite the toy cupboard.

Then Maria noticed the strangest thing.

The mice and the sofa and the table and chairs were getting larger and larger. The Christmas tree boughs reached out into the room, the needles growing much longer, and all the ornaments blowing out like balloons but keeping their various forms. The tinsel garlands were thick ropes of silver and gold. The doll's bed—and Nutcracker in it—was becoming nearly life-size. The room itself was expanding.

Or was Maria growing smaller and smaller? She felt the sofa rising beneath her. The seat was already about six feet from the floor. She had better get off right away. She slid down the curving leg, and touched the floor just a few feet from her doll's bed, which was now roomy enough for Maria herself. Nutcracker was gone!

The room was in a great commotion. The mice, as large as big dogs, were crowding together across the room, lining up in regular rows. One of them gave a high shriek, flourished his knife, and the whole band came charging toward the cupboard. Their wiry black feet made that scratchy sound Maria knew so well.

In another second the mice would have been upon her. But a bugle sounded, the cupboard door opened, and a troop of wooden soldiers as large as the mice rushed out to engage them. Cannons were wheeled into position, and ball after ball—red, pink, white, and blue—was sent in showers against the mice. But how strangely soft they were, more like big gumdrops. They seemed only to bounce off the fat mice's fur.

The bugle sounded again. A noble figure suddenly appeared at the head of the troops, in red trousers, blue coat, and plumed head dress. It was Nutcracker.

He had drawn his sword. He turned halfway round to the first line of troops, gave a command, and led them straight into the front ranks of the mouse army. What fierce hand-to-hand combat followed! The soldiers stood there bravely, but their tin swords were no match for the knives and sharp teeth of the mice.

Cranch, cranch, sounded the mouse battle-cry. Nutcracker signaled again, and the second

line of soldiers ran into the fight. Pausing a few feet from their huddled foes, they fell to their knees and took aim with their rifles. The savage mouse horde came on then, eyes and teeth flashing. The riflemen fired. Their courage was not matched by arms of sufficient power, and the shots only tickled the tough skins of the mice. One or two squealed in pain. The rest were only made more angry.

Nutcracker now summoned his last defenses. The third rank came on at a run, guns lowered and sharp steel bayonets thrust forward. The mouse villains did not move and were about to be pierced through and through when they dropped on all fours. They scampered cunningly between the soldiers' legs, unbalancing many of them, which they then carried off as prisoners.

It seemed certain now that the toy cupboard, with all its treasures, would fall victim to the mouse army. At this moment a horrible creature appeared, largest of all the mice, his terrible eyes flashing from left to right, his whiskers vibrating with rage. He wore a headdress of seven crowns. He was the Mouse King. He put himself at the front of his cutthroat band, puffed himself up with pride and prepared to lead them to the cupboard.

Nutcracker, rather badly beaten, was directly in the Mouse King's path. He stood as usual, feet planted together, holding his long, strong sword.

The Mouse King had a club—black and dreadful to look at. And he had his very large, very sharp teeth. There has never been such a strange and furious encounter. The Mouse King feigned a terrific blow with his club and then darted under his raised weapon to give his foe a savage bite. But Nutcracker was made of iron, and the Mouse King hurt his teeth so severely that he became enraged. Taking his black club in both hands, he began beating Nutcracker mercilessly. But the brave soldier warded off the club with his sword. Quickly, Nutcracker followed that with a sharp thrust at his enemy's fat belly.

But for all his fatness, the Mouse King was the quickest of the mice, and so expert at twisting and dodging and leaping and ducking this way and that, that Nutcracker could barely touch him lightly here and there. All the time he had to fend off the blows of that terrible club. Down, down, the blows kept falling on Nutcracker's head and shoulders.

Maria had been watching the combat from her place at the sofa. She saw that Nutcracker could not last much longer. But she had no gun and no sword. What could she do? Her fear for Nutcracker made her both cunning and bold. She took off one velvet slipper. No longer afraid, she ran up to the Mouse King, and as he lifted his club high over his head, she threw the slipper right in his face.

Astonished and enraged, the Mouse King deserted his opponent and raced after Maria. And that was just what she wanted.

Immediately, Nutcracker came up behind the Mouse King and struck down the monster with his sword. Maria bounced into her doll's bed. She was not hurt at all.

Nutcracker stood perfectly still for a moment. He was overcome with weariness and relief. His deep-drawn breathing was the only sound in the entire room—or was it the thudding of his heart? He put away his sword. Suddenly he topped over, without bending, like a toy.

The horde of mice, who had thought their monarch invincible, fell down in grief and terror at his death. In another moment they gathered up his swollen body in their arms, and fled. You could hear the scampering of their wiry feet, even after the last one had disappeared. Where they went, or how they went, is a mystery. All we know is that their wicked little eyes were never seen in that house again.

CHAPTER FOUR

Nutcracker stirred and opened his eyes. He raised himself on one arm. Then he stood up, restored. Restored not only to his full strength but to his true self. He was no longer dressed like a soldier: he was no longer made of iron; he no longer had a moustache and a high-arched nose. He was a handsome youth dressed in long, blue hose, a jacket and slippers of silver, and a little cloak lined with crimson. His hair was cut close, of a ruddy blond color almost matching his belt and scabbard of gold. Only his gentle eyes had not changed. They were as deep and round and confident as before.

Nutcracker crossed to the far corner of the room and found the velvet slipper that had saved his life, and then to the opposite side, where Maria's wrapper hung over the foot of the bed. He put the wrapper around her and the slipper on her foot.

"Is it you, Nutcracker?" Maria said, so astonished she could only stand and stare. "What does it all mean?"

He smiled at her very tenderly.

"It means," he said, "that the spell has been broken. I was a young boy who did

not appreciate his good fortune. I had health and friends and work to do—but I was so foolish as to be discontented and to complain of this and that all the time. An enchanter deprived me of speech and turned me into a nutcracker so that my mouth would no longer whine, but would serve some kind of purpose until I should learn to be glad of living and being of use. The spell would only be broken when someone realized how much I had changed and believed that I had a new heart under my funny costume of painted iron. It was you, Maria, who broke the enchantment— or rather, completed it. For you see, it was a lucky enchantment, since now I do know that it is good and wonderful to be alive."

The room became illuminated as the moon began to shine on the snow outside the window. It shone on Maria's slipper and on the golden sword at Nutcracker's side. It shone on all the twinkling ornaments on the Christmas tree.

"What is your real name?" Maria asked.

"My name is Prince Nikita, but now I like Nutcracker better."

"And what are you going to do now?"

"I think I shall go on being a nutcracker," he said. "That is as good a job as any, at least for a while."

"But if you are a prince you must live far away, Nutcracker. Will you go there?"

"No, I want to stay here with you, Maria. Where I live is quite far away, if you think it is far away. But it is only a few steps really. Come, I will show you."

One of the tall French windows blew open. Nutcracker lifted his beautiful sword and walked out into the night. Maria was spellbound for a moment. And then as she was about to rise and follow him, her little bed began to move like a sleigh toward the window. She tucked the wrapper and coverlet close around her. She was quite warm. Without a sound her bed glided on, under the yellow curtains, through the window, and out of doors.

Have you ever been in a forest in deep winter? With the snow frozen so hard that you

can walk on it's glassy surface, and green fir and pine trees wearing edgings of snow like white fur? With little tracks of rabbits and birds criss-crossing on the white floor, and tiny crystals of ice blinking on and off like winter fireflies? When it is so still that you can hear the least movement of twig or shifting snow?

Through such a forest Maria found herself moving in her sleighbed. Nutcracker strode on ahead, his red cloak like a beckoning torch. It was no longer night, and it was snowing again—large flakes that circled around the bed and came rushing toward it in a great throng at every new turn in the path. Then Maria saw what she had only glimpsed from the window hours ago—the Snow Fairies soaring through the air and dancing down the aisles of the forest. They were extraordinarily lovely with their costumes of silver hoarfrost and diadems of snowflakes more brilliant than diamonds. They surrounded the sleigh-bed whirling and leaping so close together that it

was quite dizzying. Then at the height of their wild dance, the forest and all its spirits seemed to melt into air.

The snow was gone. The path had become a little canal of water bordered with green plants and colorful flowers. The bed was a boat upon it. Far down the canal, Maria could see a flight of stairs at one side, with Nutcracker waiting on the lowest step. As the little boat-bed drew up, he stepped aboard beside Maria, and they sailed on.

In the distance, a castle seemed to rise out of the water. It gleamed like a giant party cake. Its walls were made of icing; over the windows were candy flowers; and peppermint stripes spiraled up the tall towers. At intervals stood statues carved out of marzipan.

An archway of golden taffy spanned the canal, and under it the boat glided into the castle. It stopped at a flight of broad steps, in a great hall made entirely of rock candy in soft pinks and yellows. A stately lady dressed in gleaming white satin stood at the top of the stairs to receive them, and beyond were many men and women dressed as if for a ball.

Nutcracker said the lady was the Sugar Plum Fairy and that this was the Fortress of Sweets. He introduced Maria, and then he told everyone how Maria had saved his life and broken the magic spell. Everyone said she had been very brave.

The Sugar Plum Fairy escorted the two children to a table overlooking the rock-candy hall. People brought in many delicious and unusual foods. For, after their battle with the mice and their trip through the forest, Nutcracker and Maria were very hungry. Each kind of refreshment was so prettily decorated that you could not tell just what it was. But it was better than ice cream, or cherry pie, or any birthday cake.

While they were eating this delectable feast, the court entertained them with music and a series of dances, each representing something good to eat or drink. Two women in ruffled skirts and two men in flaring trousers did the dance of Chocolate, which was really a Spanish dance because so much chocolate comes, or used to come, from Spain.

A stern Arab did a slow and rather sleepy dance on a rug. The music and his languid movements made you see the hot and lonely desert at night. Servants gave him tiny cups of coffee now and then, for the Arabians are great coffee drinkers.

Two Chinese girls brought in a big box of bamboo, like a tea chest. Out of it vaulted two Asian acrobats. Around and around the candy hall they turned cartwheels and flip-flops. One of the vaulted right over the table where Nutcracker and Maria were sitting. This dance was called the Dance of Tea, because the Chinese love that drink especially.

Next came a number of muscular young men dressed in red and white stripes, and carrying hoops. This was a dance of great agility and speed. The men seemed to fly through the air as they dove through their whirling hoops. It was the most brilliant dance of all.

The music changed to an airy and soaring waltz. A troop of dancers looking like flowers floated softly down from balconies and windows between the clear-sugar columns. They danced as if borne up by a breeze, and made you think of a mountain meadow. Finally, like dandelion seeds, they were wafted up, one after the other, and out between the columns.

But now came the most amusing one. How Fritz would have liked it! A very tall woman came jerkily in, wearing the most tremendous skirt, like a huge round candy box. Suddenly she lifted one part of her skirt, and out came the tiniest children, who tumbled and tripped about, just like dainty bonbons. They were dressed in pink and lavender, pale green and yellow, and there were so many of them! But somehow they all managed to crowd back under the big skirts again, and the candy-box lady sidled off.

Now the Sugar Plum Fairy came forward with a handsome man to show what they could do. And this was best of all, dancing so wonderful that Nutcracker and Maria forgot their caramel sherbet and sat enraptured.

Only a dancer could describe the grandeur and charm of those figures, responding to the music in perfect unison, creating a pattern of motion that seemed to fill the vast room with advances and retreats, vigor and grace, till you were hypnotized by its splendor. At the climax the Sugar Plum Fairy spun like a top at a furious speed all the length of the room and was caught and lifted up triumphantly by her partner.

When the applause had subsided the dancers smiled and beckoned for Nutcracker and Maria to come down. All of the court gathered around, and the children thanked them, bowing low.

CHAPTER FIVE

s Maria raised her head she knew that the court was not there. The light was different and the ballroom floor was the quilt of her bed at home. She opened her eyes wide. The clear light of the morning was streaming into her room. An icicle glittered outside the window pane, and beyond, the sky was intensely blue. There was a faint smell of toast and coffee from downstairs.

Then she saw, near the fireplace, her doll's bed. And Nutcracker lying in it, in his General's uniform. He seemed to have just awakened, too, and he was looking right at her. She thought that he smiled.

The door to the hall opened, and Maria's mother came in with a tray of food.

"How late you have slept! And on Christmas morning! The storm is over, and the whole world is washed clean. You never saw such a beautiful Christmas Day."

She came over and kissed Maria.

"I've brought you breakfast in bed, for we are all through downstairs. . . . Are you feeling well?"

"Yes, Mother, I am, and thank you for breakfast. What a party it was! . . . I was so excited I don't remember bringing Nutcracker upstairs."

"No, darling, I brought him up early this morning. And one of your slippers. The big room was in such a state . . . there were gumdrops all over the floor!"

"Mother, is Godfather Drosselmeyer a magician?"

"Of course not. He is just a clever and ingenious man who is very fond of you."

"But how did he bring Nutcracker alive?"

"If Nutcracker came alive, it was because you like him so well. If you love something very much it is always alive. . . . What a funny child you are today! Now get washed and dressed and have your breakfast. I'll light the fire."

THE END